To Nolla, who loves listening to the forest. —K.G.

For Mom and Dad, who always encourage me
to explore the world. —C.M.

22 23 24 25 26 6 5 4 3 2

Greystone Kids / Greystone Books Ltd.
greystonebooks.com

Cataloguing data available from Library and Archives Canada
ISBN 978-1-77164-736-6 (cloth)
ISBN 978-1-77164-737-3 (epub)

Editing by Tiffany Stone
Proofreading by Doeun Rivendell
Jacket and interior design by Sara Gillingham Studio

Printed and bound in China on FSC® certified paper by Shenzhen Reliance Printing.
The FSC® label means that materials used for the product have been responsibly sourced.
The illustrations in this book were rendered in gouache and color pencils, and were edited digitally.

Greystone Books thanks the Canada Council for the Arts, the British Columbia Arts Council,
the Province of British Columbia through the Book Publishing Tax Credit,
and the Government of Canada for supporting our publishing activities.

Canada

MIX
Paper from
responsible sources
FSC® C102842

BRITISH COLUMBIA | BRITISH COLUMBIA ARTS COUNCIL
An agency of the Province of British Columbia

Canada Council   Conseil des arts
for the Arts   du Canada

Greystone Books gratefully acknowledges the xʷməθkʷəy̓əm (Musqueam),
Sḵwx̱wú7mesh (Squamish), and səĺílwətaʔɬ (Tsleil-Waututh) peoples on
whose land our Vancouver head office is located.

I Hear You, Forest

Kallie George ✿ Carmen Mok

GREYSTONE KIDS

GREYSTONE BOOKS • VANCOUVER/BERKELEY/LONDON

The forest has lots to say . . .
if you listen.

Creak, creak.

I hear you, Trees,
stretching skyward.

Are you trying to tickle clouds?

Rustle, rustle.

I hear you, Leaves,
sharing secrets.

So *that's* where Robin
hides her eggs.

Croak, croak.

I hear you, Frog,
watching wide-eyed.

Who will blink first?
Oops, I did!

Trickle, trickle.

I hear you, Stream,
singing softly.

May I join and sing along?

Splish, splish.

I hear you, Deer,
drinking deeply.

I will tiptoe gently past.

Nibble, nibble.

I hear you, Squirrels,
tasting treasures.

Is it time to stop and snack?

Whoo, whoo.

I hear you, Breeze,
blowing by me.

Here's a wish to take with you.

Drip, drip.

I hear you, Dewdrops,
dancing downward.

Do you get dizzy
spinning round?

Skitter, skitter.

I hear you, Beetle,
balancing bravely.

Mama, watch what I can do!

Shhhhhhhhh.

I *see* you, Stone,
staying silent.

Are you listening, just like me?

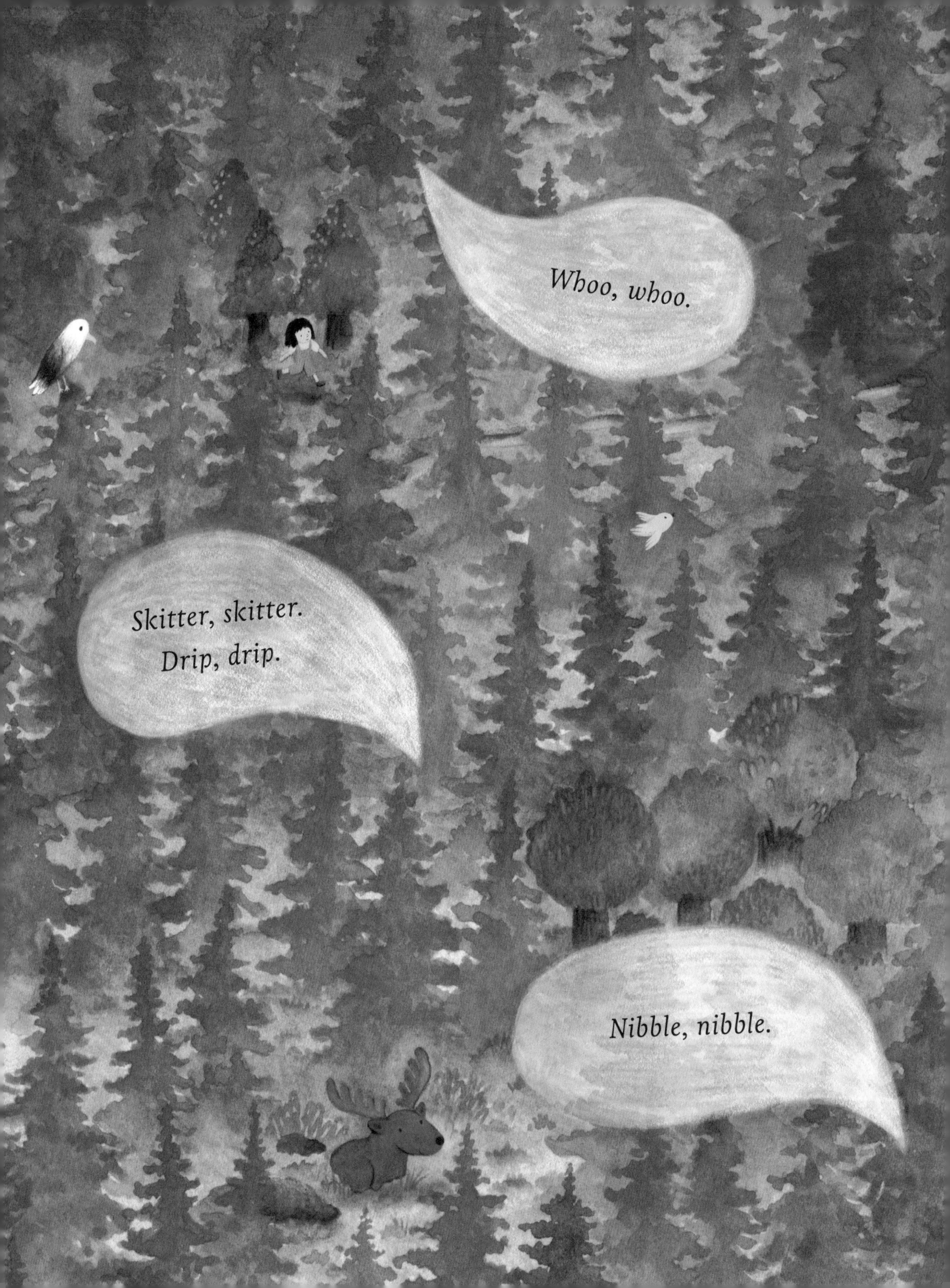
Whoo, whoo.
Skitter, skitter.
Drip, drip.
Nibble, nibble.

Splish, splish.
Trickle, trickle.
Croak, croak.
Rustle, rustle.
Creak, creak.

I hear you, Forest . . .
and all you say.

I ♥ you, Forest.